THE
BUFFALO AND
THE BELL

THE
BUFFALO

ILLUSTRATED BY *EZRA JACK KEATS*

AND
THE BELL

BY MYRA SCOVEL

FRIENDSHIP PRESS   NEW YORK

LIBRARY OF CONGRESS CATALOG CARD NUMBER: 63-8690
COPYRIGHT, © 1963, BY FRIENDSHIP PRESS, INC.
PRINTED IN THE UNITED STATES OF AMERICA

In memory of Felicia Sundar Lal

CONTENTS

1

KIRAN AND HER FAMILY

"Now, Kiran, take good care of Baby Brother," said Kiran's mother to her. "I'm glad he is asleep. I wish I did not have to leave you two here in the house alone. If only Grandfather and Aunty could have been here as we planned!" She covered her head with her scarf and walked toward the door.

It was late morning on Good Friday in a village in North India called Sherpur. Seven-year-old Kiran's mother and father were leaving to attend the three-hour service at the church in the small Christian village of Nurpur, four miles away. There wasn't any church in Kiran's village.

Grandfather was on the other side of the village with an old friend who was very sick. And of course Aunty, who looked after Grandfather, had gone with him.

"We'll be back before sundown," Mama went on.

"If you want anything, or if you are afraid to stay alone, just run across the village and get Aunty."

"Aunty would certainly be cross if I did," thought Kiran, knowing how her aunt always seemed to be angry at her.

Mama smoothed a wisp of Kiran's shining black hair into its long braid and said, "You'd better lock the street door behind us. Then go and see if Baby is awake."

Papa was already in the street, and he waved good-by to Kiran. She wanted so much to go with them, but Baby was getting heavy and four miles is a long way to walk carrying a fat baby six months old. Neighbor was not driving his bullock cart that day.

Kiran said good-by to her mother, locked the door, and went back to Baby. He was still asleep.

This was the first time that Kiran had ever been home alone. She told herself that she wasn't exactly afraid. But she decided to look into all the rooms around their courtyard anyway, just to be sure that everything was all right.

The sun was bright as she crossed the courtyard again. But the long narrow room in front was dark and cool. This was the room where Papa and Grandfather talked with the men who came to see them. Kiran saw that the street door was still bolted, as Mama had said before she left.

She went back into the courtyard, glancing into the shed on her left where the buffalo slept. She liked the smell of the buffalo's shed. She wished Old Buffalo were home so she wouldn't feel quite so alone, but Old Buffalo was out in the fields, grazing.

Across the courtyard, just in front of Kiran, was Grandfather's house. She could see the heavy chain with its padlock hanging against the wooden doors. Kiran went back into her own house and sat down on the earthen floor. There was no need to look into Young Uncle's small house across the courtyard. It had been closed and locked for a long time. Young Uncle was away in the Indian army and his pretty little wife had gone to live at her mother's home in the village to the north. Kiran missed her because Young Uncle's wife had often played with her.

Now Kiran had no one to play with. There were boys her own age among their few Christian neighbors, but Kiran was the only little girl in the small section of the village where the Christians lived. The boys all played *Kubuddi*, but girls were not allowed to play such rough games. Kiran laughed to herself even to think of such a thing as girls playing *Ku-*

buddi. Imagine two teams of girls running back and forth, with one girl shouting, *"Kubuddi, kubuddi, kubuddi, kubuddi,"* until her breath ran out and she could be tagged! And in front of the whole village, too! Girls were meant for inside the house, not for the playing field.

"Sometimes I wish I were a boy," thought Kiran. "Every family in this village wants boys. Girls cost too much because when a girl gets married her father has to give a lot of money to her husband's family. Baby is a boy, and since he came to our family, nobody pays any attention to me." Then Kiran thought about her name, and she knew her family didn't really feel that way about her. Kiran meant "a ray of light."

Her parents had often said to her, "A ray of light entered our home when you came to us, Kiran." Papa and Mama had never let anyone feel sorry for them because they had a girl child. God had sent her to them, they would say, and they were happy with their little Ray of Light.

Kiran got up and went to the door of her house. The weather was hot and the sky was like brass. It would be three long months before the monsoon winds came with their cooling rains. Hot, hot weather and nothing to do—not one thing for Kiran to do.

The baby began to stir in his sleep. Baby was a nuisance anyway! Kiran remembered what it was like before Baby came. She had been the only child. Papa and Mama had never left her at home then. They took her everywhere with them, or they stayed at home with her.

Then suddenly one day, Mama had gone to her home village and Kiran and Papa were left alone. The house seemed strange without Mama. They ate all their meals with Grandfather and Aunty. Aunty was cross and irritable, and Kiran missed her mother's soft voice and kindly way of doing things. When bedtime came, she missed Mama most of all. She missed the close little circle at family prayers. Papa's voice when he read the Bible had a dull wooden sound, not at all like Mama's rich, happy voice as she read and prayed. But Kiran loved Papa very much and she liked being with him. So the days passed.

Then, as suddenly as she had gone, Mama had arrived back in the village. Mama had a small bundle in her arms, which she said was a gift for Kiran. But the bundle had been a little brother—and he was no gift to her at all.

The whole neighborhood seemed to own him. Such a fuss as everyone made that day!

"A boy at last! A boy at last!" their Hindu neighbors had said. And Papa and Mama had looked so proud and so happy.

"But now they never ask me to sing any more," Kiran thought as she went over to the bed to see if Baby were awake. "Before Baby came, Mama and Papa would always ask me to sing songs for the neighbors. Now all that anybody wants to do is to look at the baby. Oh, how I wish he had never, never come into our home!"

Baby began to cry. Mama would be gone for more than three hours. What would she do with this crying baby? Perhaps she could hide him in the clumps of tall grass near the canal. She knew just such a secret place. She sometimes played there in the late afternoon while waiting to take their buffalo home when the herd boy brought the village animals in from grazing.

How Kiran disliked that herd boy! "He is mean to everyone, and especially mean to me," thought Kiran. "When I take our buffalo out to join the herd for grazing, he drives his buffalo straight toward me and I have to run to get out of the way!"

The boy's name was Ganga Ram, and he was the son of Bishan Das, the Chief Elder of the village. Ganga Ram's legs were so badly crippled that he could not stand. Someone had to lift him onto the buffalo's back so that he could drive the village animals out to where the sweet grass grew. Everyone felt sorry for his father, Bishan Das, though he was the richest man in the village. Bishan Das was a Hindu. The Christians and the Hindus did not always get along well together, but all the Christians liked Bishan Das. This son of his, Ganga Ram, was not like his father.

"I don't like that herd boy at all," said Kiran to herself. "I don't like the way he grins. I don't like the sloppy way his turban comes undone. I don't like his spindly legs hanging over the buffalo's back. I don't like anything about him."

Baby cried louder and louder. Kiran picked him up and walked through the courtyard to the street door. Hardly thinking what she was doing, she unbolted it and walked down the road toward the canal. She turned off onto the little path that led to her special hiding place.

As she walked, the baby became quiet, and she noticed that he had fallen asleep again. "I'll just lay him here on this tuft of coarse grass," she said to herself. The tuft had been cut for making baskets, and the grass around it grew up higher than Kiran's head. No one would find a sleeping baby here. Kiran covered him with his blanket and ran home as fast as she could.

"Now," said Kiran as she went back into the house, "with Baby out of the way, I can have the whole place to myself."

She took out her clay dishes and began to play with them. She would arrange a tea party for Mama and Papa and herself, just the three of them—the kind of pretend party that the three of them used to play before Baby came.

"I wonder if he is awake and crying," she thought. "Well, let him cry. I am not going to think about him." She laid the dishes out on the low stool that would serve as a table. Then she took a handful of bright yellow millet seeds and dropped a few of them into each of the clay cups.

But Kiran couldn't stop thinking about Baby. What was he doing now? Perhaps he was frightened lying out there all alone. What would Mama say? And what would Papa say? Would he be as angry as he had been that day the rent collector beat their neighbor's boy so hard? She would not like to have Papa look at her as he had looked at the rent collector that day. Perhaps she had better go back and see how Baby was. He might be awake now.

16

She hurried down the road, and there she met the old woman whom everyone in the village called "Old Grandmother." Old Grandmother was hobbling along, pounding her stick on the road. She was on her way to the Good Friday service. Old Grandmother was late as she always was—very late this time. She had probably been stopped by someone who wanted advice. A great many people turned to Old Grandmother when they needed help. She lived in the village two miles the other side of Kiran's village, Sherpur. She would still have to walk from Sherpur to Nurpur. But she stopped to talk with Kiran.

"Kiran, little one, why aren't you at worship with the rest of the family?" she asked.

"I stayed at home to look after the baby," said Kiran. Old Grandmother was a little deaf, and Kiran had to shout.

"You stayed at home to look after the baby? Well, where is the baby? You haven't left him all alone to fall into the fire?" asked Old Grandmother, peering anxiously at Kiran.

"He is asleep on the bed and there is no fire," lied Kiran. "I thought I'd just run out to see how the buffalo is. She did not seem well this morning when I took her out to the herd."

"Good girl! You think of everything and everyone, Kiran. Come near and I will give you my blessing." She placed her old, gnarled hands on Kiran's head and said, "God bless you and keep you. In Jesus' name, Amen."

Old Grandmother walked on and Kiran hurried toward the place where she had hidden Baby. Her head felt hot where Old Grandmother's hands had lain. Usually she loved Old Grandmother's blessings.

They always seemed to mean something special. "God make you beautiful without and within," Old Grandmother had prayed one day, and Kiran had felt beautiful every time she thought of it. Today she felt ugly.

She looked up at the sky. A hot wind had begun to blow and swirls of sand were moving toward her. Suppose Baby should get the coughing sickness and die as Ram Singh's baby had died? She ran as fast as she could run and soon found the mound of grass. Yes, there lay the blanket. She turned back the corner, but Baby was not there! Had some wild animal taken him? She tried to call out, but she couldn't speak. She tried to run for help, but she couldn't move.

"Oh, God, help me," she sobbed, falling on her knees. "Why did I do it?"

She felt a tug at her trouser leg. Had the animal come back after her? She was afraid to open her eyes. Again the tug. Then she thought she heard Baby's cooing. She opened one eye and there was Baby, safe and sound, playing beside her and smiling up at her. He wasn't lost at all. He had just crawled off the mound of grass onto the ground.

She took him in her arms and hugged him and hugged him. She wrapped the blanket around him, saying, "O, thank you, God, thank you! I'm so glad you didn't let anything happen to him. I'll never stop loving him all my life."

Baby stuck his chubby little fist into her hair and gave it a good pull.

When Mama and Papa got home, they found Kiran and the baby playing together. Baby had Kiran's precious clay teapot in his hands and would soon have it in his mouth.

"Don't let him break your teapot," Mama warned as she came in the door.

Mama was in such a hurry to get supper that she hardly looked at Kiran. Kiran watched her as she took her long muslin scarf from across her shoulders and tied it around her waist so it would not fall into the fire. Mama tucked up her green tunic that fell like a skirt below her knees, pulled up her wide green trousers, and squatted down to fan the fire on the hearth to a bright blue flame.

Papa had been talking when he came in the door, and he went on in his slow deliberate way. "I wish the new church could have been completed in time for Easter," he said.

"You're lucky to have this much of the building finished. What with the spring harvest and all, you men haven't been out of the fields long enough to eat and sleep," said Mama. She patted the *chapatti* dough into a flat pancake and laid it on the small iron dome that she had set over the fire to heat. Kiran always liked the smell of *chapatties*.

"It is good of the city pastor to bring his young people out to help us build the rest of the church," said Papa. "With so many working, we can get a lot done in a few days. There'll be benches to make, plastering to do, the yard to clean—Kiran, you and the other children can help with that. It's too bad that the work couldn't have been done this week, so we could have the church all finished by Easter."

"The young men and women couldn't have come from the city before their school vacation anyway," said Mama. She lifted the *chapatti* off the dome with her tongs and plopped it into the ashes, where it began to puff up into a crisp ball.

All this talk about the new church! "Oh, I wish they'd be quiet so I could tell them what I did today," thought Kiran. "I know they will be angry with me. I don't want to tell Mama and Papa what I did to Baby, but I must."

But Mama and Papa talked all through the meal. They talked about the young missionary architect who had come from the city some years before to draw plans for the new church. Kiran had been quite little then, but she remembered him. They had gone to Nurpur in Neighbor's cart. There had been a service of worship outdoors on the land where the new church was to be built. Afterward Kiran had watched the young missionary as he drew plans on large sheets of paper. Kiran had watched him draw the belfry.

"What is that?" she had asked. "It looks like a little church on top of a big one."

"It is the place where a bell will hang," the missionary architect had told her. "The bell will ring out over the fields and everyone who hears it will want to come to church."

Kiran thought it would be fun to hear a bell ringing and ringing, but now as she listened to Mama and Papa, she knew there wouldn't be a new bell for a long, long time—maybe never.

"We still haven't enough money to buy that bell," Papa was saying. "I don't see how any of us can give any more money toward it this year."

All the Christian families had given as much as they could. There wouldn't be any new clothes for any of them to wear in the procession to the church on Easter morning. Kiran had wanted a new tunic and trousers to match. But Mama told her all their money should go for the new bell for the church. In the end Kiran asked Papa to give her clothes money for the new bell, too. Sometimes it was hard not to wish she had chosen the new clothes instead.

Now Kiran looked from one to the other of her parents as she held Baby in her arms and ate her *chapatti*. Somehow the hot bread didn't taste very good tonight. She wished that Mama or Papa would look at her, that one of them would say, "You look sad, Kiran. What is troubling our little girl?" Then she could tell them what she had done to Baby. Baby was laughing up at her now as if nothing had happened that afternoon. Kiran wished she could forget it as easily.

Papa drank his tea and then got up. "I think I'll go across the village and see that Grandfather gets home all right," he said. "He and Aunty may need a little help. I'll pick up Old Buffalo on my way back. I told Ganga Ram to leave her with Neighbor until I got home."

"Let's not hurry with the cleaning up," said Mama to Kiran after Papa left. She took Baby from Kiran and went out through the courtyard to the street door. "Come, Kiran," she called. "Let's look out for a minute. I love this time of day."

She put her arm around Kiran's shoulders, and from the doorway the two watched the farmers and their bullocks coming in from the fields. Lavender shadows cast by the trees played across the sides of the animals as they plodded along. Shafts of late sunlight made sparkles of gold from the dust that sifted up from the dirt road. The peacocks were flying in from the fields to perch in the trees for the night. Everything was quiet and full of peace.

"Mama, I want to tell you something," said Kiran.

2

KIRAN TELLS

"What is it you want to tell me, Kiran?" asked Mama.

The longer Kiran waited to tell Mama she had hidden Baby in the grass, the harder it became for her to say anything. Then, just as she started to tell her story, they heard the thumping of a stick coming around the corner of their house. It was Old Grandmother.

"Now just what are you two doing here at this time of day, I'd like to know," Old Grandmother said. "You've probably had a cold supper and are all finished by now. And I'm not even home yet."

Old Grandmother must have stopped to talk to each one of her friends, to be this late getting home.

"Come in and rest a while, Old Grandmother," said Mama. "You look tired. I know you still have two miles to go, but please stop long enough for some tea."

"No, I really mustn't," said Old Grandmother. "Your fire is out and I cannot wait while you go to the neighbor's for a burning coal to build a new one."

"But, Old Grandmother, our fire is not out. Come in and see. The water is boiling," said Mama.

"That's funny. I met Kiran on the road going to see the sick buffalo and she said the fire was out," said Old Grandmother as they walked into the house.

Now what would Mama say? Kiran knew she had lied to Old Grandmother. She remembered what the pastor had said in one of his sermons to the children.

"Children, if you tell one lie, you will have to tell many lies to make things seem right, and each lie is like a strong string. Soon you will be caught in your own lies as a fish is caught in a net."

Kiran followed her mother and Old Grandmother into the house and sat down on the floor, wishing with all her heart that Old Grandmother would leave. But now Old Grandmother was talking about the new church bell. "Can't anybody in this house think of anything except that church and its bell?" Kiran said to herself.

"I just don't see the need of a bell for a church," Old Grandmother was saying. "The Christians in these villages need a lot of other things besides bells."

"The men say that it will call us all to worship," Mama replied. "When the bell first rings, we'll know it is time to leave our homes and start our journey to the church. When the bell rings again, we will know it is time to begin worship."

"A lot of good that'll do me," said Old Grandmother. "Me—deaf as a post and six miles away. I get there when I can get there, and that's all there is to it!"

"I never thought that you might not be able to hear it as far away as your village," said Mama. "The men say that here in our village those who are not Christians will hear the bell. Then they will want to come and see what all the ringing is about. I am sure that if only they could hear the wonderful story of Jesus, they would give their hearts to him."

"That may be, that may be," said Old Grandmother. She patted Baby as Mama rocked him in her arms. Kiran watched the expression on Mama's face as she bent over Baby.

"Old Grandmother, he is so precious," said Mama. "I am always afraid that something will happen to him. So many babies in the village have died, and it seems to happen so many times in families where there is only one boy."

"Nonsense!" said Old Grandmother. "God has given

you a good son and a good daughter. Your daughter is just as precious as your son. Trust the Heavenly Father to care for both of them. Such worry and such thinking on your part is not good. It shows that you are putting too much thought upon your son. You have a lot for which to be thankful in having such a lovely daughter. What a thoughtful child she is—going out to see the sick buffalo!"

Just then Papa came into the house. "What's this about a sick buffalo?" he asked. "I hadn't heard about any sick buffalo in the village. Heaven knows there is trouble enough—not too good a spring harvest, and all the money promised to the church. Now if the buffaloes are getting sick, we will be in a fix!"

Kiran trembled. She was caught in the net of the lie she had made, just as Pastor had said she would be.

"There is nothing to worry about," said Mama. "We women were just talking. Here, Papa, have your tea."

"Doesn't he know that his buffalo is sick?" whispered Old Grandmother.

"No, he doesn't," said Mama. "Old Grandmother, you are very tired. Why not stay here for the next two nights? Then you can go with us to Nurpur for the Easter sunrise service. Perhaps we can get Neighbor to take you in his cart."

"That is very thoughtful of you," said Old Grandmother. "I'd like to stay, but I must not worry the family. They would think that something terrible had happened to me if I did not come home tonight."

"Now, Old Grandmother, you must stay," said Papa. "Sher Singh has brought his plow over to our blacksmith. I'll catch him before he goes back to your village and he can tell your famiy that you are staying with us. They'll surely be going to the service at Nur-

pur on Sunday morning. We will wait for them here and all leave together in the Easter procession to Nur-pur."

"Yes, of course, they'll be going to the Easter service. Since you've planned it so well, I think I'll stay," said Old Grandmother.

Kiran was miserable. With Old Grandmother here all the time, she could never forget for a moment what she had done to Baby. Old Grandmother would keep talking about the sick buffalo and no fire. Worst of all, Kiran could not have a quiet talk with Mama.

When Papa came back from the blacksmith shop, they gathered for prayers. Mama read from the Bible. Papa and Kiran both liked to have Mama read because she knew the words so well and made them sound so beautiful. Kiran was proud that her mother could read. Most of the mothers in the village could not read at all. Mama had learned to read before she was married. A Bible woman had taught Mama in her home. What was she reading now?

"As far as the east is from the west, so far does he remove our transgressions from us."

How good it would be to feel that what she had done today could be pushed as far away from her as the western sky she and Mama had seen from the front door! Kiran wanted with all her heart to tell what she had done to Baby, so the heavy ache inside her would go away. Kiran always told Mama everything, perhaps because the two of them were alone in the house so much of the time. But, oh, Kiran did not want Papa to know! She did not want to see that stern look in his eyes.

But Kiran was certainly not going to tell, in front of Old Grandmother, the whole story of what she had done to Baby. Nor about the buffalo that was not sick and the fire that was not out.

While they were all kneeling, Kiran prayed, "Oh, God, I don't want to tell Mama and Papa, but if I must tell them, help me to do it."

As they rose from their knees, Old Grandmother said, "I think I'll run in and say good night to Kiran's grandfather. It wouldn't do for me to visit this home without paying my respects to the head of the family." Papa went with her to light the way.

"Oh, Mama, you will hate me!" Kiran sobbed, as she threw herself into her mother's arms. In a few minutes the whole story had been blurted out. Kiran told of wanting Mama and Papa to pay attention to her, of how she had taken Baby out to the field and left him there, of how frightened she had been when she couldn't find him. Then Kiran looked up into her mother's face.

Mama was quiet—very, very quiet for a long, long time. At last she said, "Kiran, how could you have done such a terrible thing? Leaving Baby out there all alone! Oh, I shudder even to think of what might have happened to him."

Mama had been looking at Baby as he lay on her bed. Now she turned to Kiran. "But perhaps Old Grandmother was right when she said that I have been paying too much attention to our little boy. I have been so busy taking care of Baby that I haven't shown you how much I love you. I never told you about him beforehand, and I didn't prepare you in any way for Baby's coming into our family. Let us kneel down and ask God to forgive us both."

As they knelt, Kiran felt Mama's arm clasped tightly around her shoulders. She knew, after they had prayed together, that God had pushed her sin over the edge of the western skyline.

"Mama, will you tell Papa?" asked Kiran.

"Yes, Kiran, I will try to tell him," said Mama.

Mama went over to the hearth to cover the coals with ash so that they would keep glowing until it was time to cook breakfast. Kiran heard her mother say to herself, "So that was why Old Grandmother kept talking about no fire and the sick buffalo. I thought her brain was getting muddled."

Soon Kiran fell asleep, exhausted from the worries of the day. In the night she awakened and saw Papa bending over her. He was tucking the blanket around her shoulders. "Poor little girl," he was saying. "Poor little girl."

3

KIRAN PLANS A PRESENT

Kiran woke up early next morning. She lay on her small string cot and thought about Easter. As she thought, she ran her fingers over the heavy cord that Mama had woven so tightly into red and white squares to make a firm bed for Kiran to lie on.

Tomorrow would be such a happy day! She remembered last Easter, when she wore her new pink trousers and tunic with the deep red scarf. It had been so much fun to peep through the scarf when she covered her head in church. It made the whole church seem a beautiful rose color. This Easter she would have to wear the same clothes. No one in the Christian families of Nurpur would have anything new to wear in the Easter procession.

Still, it would be fun to wait with her family at the door of their home until the Christians from Old Grandmother's village came down the street on their way to Nurpur. She would hear them, long before she could see them, singing songs of praise as they walked along the road. The drum would be thrumping the familiar rhythm that Kiran loved. She hoped that they all might sing together the hymn Mama had taught her—"He is risen! Christ is risen! Sing, ye happy people, sing!" If they sang this hymn, she would not mind the long walk to Nurpur.

Kiran always liked to go to Nurpur. Her village, Sherpur, meant "The Village of Lions," but Nurpur meant "The Village of Light." All of the people in Nurpur were Christians. In Nurpur, one didn't always have to be afraid of bumping into a Hindu person of high caste. If a Christian touched a Hindu, the Hindu became furious. Hindus thought Christians were unclean. In Nurpur people could eat together and drink water from the same wells. But it was not the same in their own village of Sherpur. Here the Christians had to live apart and were looked down upon. They could not touch the wells from which the Hindus drank. Papa kept saying that things would be better now because the government of India considered all men equal, but it seemed to take a long time for the people in the village of Sherpur to treat the Christians as brothers.

Even with the singing and the drums it would be a long walk to Nurpur. And this year Baby would be in church with them. Why, just think! It would be Baby's first Easter! Papa had said last night that Baby would ride to Nurpur in Neighbor's cart with Grandfather and Old Grandmother.

"I wish I could buy Baby an Easter present," thought Kiran. "After what I did to him yesterday, I'd like to do something to show him how much I love him."

The family were waking now. Papa was just coming in from the covered veranda where he had been sleeping on the cool earthen floor. Mama was getting up. Baby had started to whimper. Old Grandmother gave a final snore. Kiran rose and picked Baby up so that Mama could get breakfast.

After they had had family prayers and had finished their meal, Kiran helped Mama polish the brass trays they used as plates. Then Mama let her arrange them against the back of the shelves built into the kitchen wall. Kiran placed the large tray in the middle and the smaller ones on each side. Then she put the bowls in front of the brass plates. She stepped back to look at the pretty arrangement she had made.

All this time she had been wondering how she could buy Baby an Easter present. She couldn't ask Mama and Papa for money because she knew they didn't have any. Besides, this had to be Kiran's own gift to Baby.

She took up the large clay pot and put it on her head to carry it to the village well. "How can I get some money—even a little money?" she was thinking. When she got to the well, she filled her jar without talking to any of the women who were there. She balanced the heavy jar on her head and started back down the road. As she kicked the dust with her bare feet, her anklet bells sang a pretty little tinkly song. Then, just as she got to the door of her house, Kiran had an idea. She would sell her anklet.

Kiran walked past the room where the buffalo slept, crossed the courtyard, and went into the kitchen where Mama was. She set down her water jar and hurried out to take Old Buffalo down to meet Ganga Ram, the herd boy. She didn't want to be late this morning, for then she would have to take the buffalo out to the grazing field herself.

But it was a good day, a very good day. Old Buffalo ran on ahead and joined the herd all by herself, and Kiran didn't have to be teased by Ganga Ram because he had already passed their corner and didn't see her. She ran back to the house to see what else Mama wanted her to do.

Old Grandmother was not there. She had probably gone to see one of the neighbors. But Aunty had come in. Aunty and Mama had come from the same village before they were married. Now they were laughing together, as they always did, recalling the things they did together when they were young. Kiran wished she knew a little girl her own age to be best friends with.

"Whoever thought, years ago, that you and I would be cooking together in the same kitchen?" Aunty was saying. "Weren't we lucky to be chosen as brides in the same family? Remember? We almost didn't get chosen. We could both read. So they thought we had too much education to make good farmers' wives. As it was, I had to give up my nurse's training, just when I had almost finished it.

"You haven't enough *ghee*, butter fat, to fry all these sweets," Aunty went on. "I'll run over and get some of ours." She brushed past Kiran on her way out.

"Cross old Aunty, who would choose her as a wife?" wondered Kiran.

"Mama, who was Aunty's husband?" she asked.

"Why, darling, didn't you know? He was Papa's brother, the one between Papa and Young Uncle. I'm sure we told you!" said Mama.

"Where is he now?" asked Kiran.

"He is dead, Kiran. Aunty has had a very great unhappiness," said Mama. She suddenly stopped talking. Aunty was coming in the door, holding in her hands a large tin can filled with melted butter fat.

"Kiran," said Aunty crossly, "get out of my way. Don't just stand there with your mouth open. Do you want me to spill this *ghee*?"

"She is so happy with Mama and so cross with me. I wonder why," thought Kiran.

"You may go over to see Grandfather, Kiran," said Mama kindly. "Aunty and I must cook the sweets for Easter. All the other work is done."

Usually Kiran begged to help her mother make the sweets. She loved to watch the golden oil bubble and break as the cakes danced in the brass pot. She loved to hear the little hissing song the cakes sang as they were taken from the hot oil and placed on the cold brass tray. But today she hurried out of the door and went around to the back of the house where no one could see her.

Kiran sat down under a tree and tried and tried to take off her anklet, but it had been there so long that it was too tight to slip off. Now she couldn't go to Grandfather's. She would have to go down the street

to Uncle Blacksmith, who was a Christian, and ask
him to cut off her brass anklet. Then she could sell it
to the secondhand man at the corner of the bazaar.
She would spend whatever he gave her to buy Baby
his gift.

When she reached the blacksmith shop, she found
men crowded around the fire, talking and bargaining
for the repair of tools or plows, or buying rings for
their oxen's harnesses.

"Uncle Blacksmith, sir," said Kiran. But he paid no
attention to her.

"So, you Christians are getting swelled heads, are
you?" the fat moneylender was saying. "Not content
with your new church, you must now have a bell."

"Let him alone," said Bishan Das, the Hindu village
elder. "The Christians have done well. The bell will
ring to the glory of God.

"Here is money for the plow," he said to the blacksmith, "and here is more to add to the fund you are
collecting for the bell."

Even here at the blacksmith shop, people were talking about that bell! Why couldn't someone pay a little
attention to her!

Kiran tried to wait until all the men had gone, but
every time the small crowd thinned out, another man

would arrive with new requests. At last Uncle Blacksmith noticed her. He looked at her sternly and said, "Kiran, you run along home. A blacksmith shop is no place for a little girl."

Kiran was almost in tears. She knew that girls should not be seen in a crowd of men, but she didn't like to have the blacksmith tell her so. And how else could she get her anklet cut off? She walked along the village street slowly. She looked up at the sky and saw that the sun was directly overhead. "It is noon," she thought. "I must hurry home before Mama misses me."

When she got to the corner where the secondhand man lived, she saw that the wooden doors of his shop were closed and the huge brass padlock was securely fastened. The secondhand man must have left the village for a day or two. Even if she could get her anklet off, she would not be able to sell it.

Kiran slipped in at the doorway of her home. She didn't want to talk to anyone. She was glad Baby was asleep on Mama's string bed. Mama and Aunty were chattering away as the oil bubbled and the cakes sang, but Kiran didn't feel like watching them. Tomorrow was Easter and she had wanted so much to buy Baby an Easter present.

4

OLD BUFFALO AND THE BEADS

Suddenly the dogs outside set up a furious barking and Kiran ran out to see who was coming. It was Young Uncle in his army uniform!

"How is my favorite niece?" he asked, lifting Kiran off the ground. "Oh, but you have grown since I last saw you!"

Mama and Aunty dropped everything and ran to greet Young Uncle.

"I can stay only a few hours," he told them. "I must go on to Rajpur before night."

Rajpur was his wife's village, where she was staying with her parents while Young Uncle was away.

"Kiran, dear, run out to the fields and call your father to come while I make some tea," said Mama.

"And here, Favorite Niece, are eight annas. Buy yourself something as you go through the bazaar," said Young Uncle. Then he turned to Mama and

Aunty. "I'll hurry in to see Father. Call us when you get that tea made." And he started across the courtyard toward Grandfather's house.

Kiran stood looking at the coin in her hand. Everything had happened so suddenly that she was stunned. Eight annas! Why that was half a rupee! She had never before held so much money in her hand.

"Kiran, your mother told you to go to the field and call your father," said Aunty sternly. "Don't just stand there. Go and do as she said."

"Run along, darling," said Mama. "Young Uncle really shouldn't have given you so much money."

Kiran's bracelets and anklet sang the quick rhythm of a song as she ran toward the fields for her father. Eight annas! With all this money, she could buy a wonderful present for Baby.

The field where Papa was working was on the other side of the village, and Kiran slowed her pace as she came to the bazaar. What could she buy for Baby? A woven basket? Baby couldn't play with a basket. He was too small. Ah, a bright red stool with a green and yellow string seat! But, no, Baby would get tired sitting on a stool without a back. And besides, he'd probably fall off. A string of brass bells to put around his ankle? Baby was a boy—anklets were for girls,

She came up to a wooden cart standing by the edge of the road. Combs, thread, snaps, needles, jars of hair cream, dishes, and toys were piled high. Here was a big rubber ball, but Baby's hands were too small to hold such a big ball, and the celluloid toys would be too easily broken. What could she find for Baby?

She was almost out of the village when she passed the harness shop. There, hanging on the post that held up the roof, were strings of large, bright-colored beads, made for the animals to wear around their necks on feast days. A string of donkey beads! That would be just the gift for Baby. Baby liked bright colors, and he loved to suck smooth things. The beads would be a wonderful toy for Baby to play with. When he got bigger, Kiran would teach him how to string the beads in different arrangements of colors. She chose a string of blue, white, red, and black ones.

"How much are these?" she asked the harness seller at the shop door.

"Twelve annas," the old man replied.

"That is too much," said Kiran, bargaining as she had been taught. "See, here are two beads with chips in them. I will give you eight annas for the string."

"So, the child is teaching the man! If you do not like my chipped beads, go to another shop," he said.

"Oh, Grandfather Harness Man," said Kiran respectfully, "I have only eight annas and I want to buy an Easter present for Baby."

"So Baby is a donkey," said the harness man, "and must wear a string of donkey beads around his neck!"

"But these are not for wearing, Grandfather," said Kiran. "These are for Baby to play with. Please give them to me for eight annas."

"Yes, yes, take them for eight annas. No wonder I am such a poor man. My heart is so soft and kind. Take them, take them," said the old man.

Kiran ran off happily, knowing that he had intended to sell them for eight annas all the time.

As she walked along, she wondered where she would hide them when she got home. She didn't want Baby to see them until Easter morning. Finally she decided to tuck them between the woven strings in the corner of her bed as soon as she got home.

As Kiran crossed the little bridge over the canal, she saw the village buffaloes soaking themselves in the water. Their own buffalo was just beneath the bridge where Kiran stood. The only part of her Kiran could see were her curved horns, her eyes, and her snout.

"I wonder where Papa is working," Kiran thought, as she stood on the bridge scanning the fields. There the men were, in the north field. Papa had already seen her and was waving to her. As she lifted her arm to wave back, the beads slipped off her arm, fell into the water with a splash, and disappeared.

"Oh no, oh no!" cried Kiran.

Kiran ran to her father. "Oh, Papa, I've lost my beads in the water, and Young Uncle has come home, and Mama wants me to call you and now I have no Easter present for Baby, and my money is all gone, too!" wailed Kiran.

"What are you talking about?" asked Papa. "You haven't any money to lose and your necklace is still around your neck and Young Uncle is miles away."

"No, no, no, he is here and it is not my necklace but the donkey beads," said Kiran between sobs.

"Donkey beads? It is a donkey head you have," said Papa. "Here, sit down and tell me all about it."

They sat down together at the edge of the field under the trees of the mango grove, and as she nestled close to her father, she told him the whole sad story.

"Don't cry," said Papa. He took the end of Kiran's scarf and dried her eyes. "I'll wade into the water and see if I can find them with a stick." He broke off a dead branch, and they went back to the canal.

Papa waded into the water as far as he could, but

the water under the bridge was deep and he feared that the beads had been swept downstream. He fished around with the stick but found nothing.

"I'm sorry, Daughter," said Papa. "I know what we will do. I'll help you make something for Baby. We'll find a good piece of wood and I'll carve a wooden buffalo for him."

"Baby would love a carved buffalo," Kiran replied,

"but, Papa, that would be your present to Baby. It wouldn't be my present at all."

"It will be our present, yours and mine," said Papa, "because I would not have thought of an Easter present for Baby if it hadn't been for you."

He and Kiran stood for a minute watching Old Buffalo. "There's nothing sick about you, is there, Old Healthy One," said Papa. The buffalo gave a snort and

heaved herself out of the water. Kiran and Papa burst out laughing. There, strung crazily across the horns of the buffalo and down over one eye, was the beautiful string of donkey beads, glistening in the sunlight!

"They must have fallen on Old Buffalo's neck when I waved to you from the bridge," said Kiran. "Our buffalo was right there when the beads fell into the water."

Papa and Kiran walked home together, singing a song of praise. It was the lilting happy song that Kiran hoped they would be singing as they joined the Christians in their Easter procession tomorrow at sunrise. "He is risen! Christ is risen! Sing, ye happy people, sing!"

"Papa," said Kiran, "do you think the new bell will be ready for next Easter?"

"I certainly hope we won't have to wait any longer than that," said Papa.

"It will be fun to walk to Nurpur again," said Kiran. "Do you remember the time we met the big elephant coming down the road and how frightened I was of the *sadhu* who was leading him?"

"Indeed I do," said Papa. "I had to carry you for two long miles. I don't wonder you were frightened—all that paint on his body and his hair so long and

50

matted. But I suppose he thinks God wants him to be that way. Kiran, you don't know how thankful you should be that you know the story of Jesus and his love for us."

They were turning the corner into their street.

"When we go to Nurpur this time," said Papa, "we will be staying for a few days."

"Staying at Nurpur? What do you mean?" Kiran asked.

"Wait until we get home and I will tell all of you together," said Papa with a smile.

They found the rest of the family in the inner courtyard, seated around the doorway. All the family were there except Grandfather, who didn't like the noise of a lot of talking.

Kiran hurried into the house and hid her gift for Baby in the corner of her string bed. Then she went back to the courtyard. She wanted so much to hear about their staying at Nurpur, but Papa was talking with Young Uncle and they were all drinking their tea. Kiran passed the Easter sweets.

At last Papa said, "We men talked it over as we worked today. We've decided that two or three of the families from our village here should stay in Nurpur after Easter to help the young people work on the new church. I have promised that our family will be one of those to help. Mama and Kiran and Baby and Aunty can stay with Mama's cousin there. Grandfather will stay with the pastor, and I'm sure there will be some corner where he can tuck me in, too. Then I'll be on hand to help him early in the morning before the city pastor arrives with his students."

For a few minutes everyone was talking at once. Students from the city! Staying in Nurpur! The church finished! Kiran could hardly wait for tomorrow to come.

5

GRANDFATHER'S STORY

After Kiran heard the news about staying in Nurpur for four days, she was so excited she had to tell somebody about it. But whom would she tell? Kiran used to tell Young Uncle's wife all the exciting and sad things that happened, but now Young Uncle's wife was far away in her home village.

"I wish there were some little girl my age around here," thought Kiran. "Why do we have to have so many boys in our section of the village?"

It was hot in the courtyard, and the grownups were talking about crops and money. She would go into Grandfather's house and talk with him. Kiran loved Grandfather's house. The walls were thicker and the ceilings were higher than in her own house, and that made it cooler than the small rooms in Kiran's house.

As she stopped to run her fingers over the wood carving on Grandfather's doorway, Aunty called out

from where she was sitting with the rest of the grownups, "Kiran, take your shoes off before you go in. I will
not have you getting dirt on the rug that your grandmother made with her own hands. And don't chatter
every minute. Grandfather is tired."

"Who's tired?" It was Grandfather's voice and it
came from the bedroom.

Kiran slipped off her sandals and went through the main room into Grandfather's room. Grandfather was sitting by the open square in the wall that served as a window. He took off his steel-rimmed glasses, which were really only half glasses. He placed the worn Bible he had been reading on the window ledge and set his glasses upon it. Then he turned to Kiran.

"Well, Kiran," he said, "what is the news? Excitement is bursting out all over you like air escaping from a balloon. You're bouncing around just like a balloon, too. Sit down here beside me and tell me all about it. It's good to see you, child. Nobody comes to see old Grandfather any more unless he wants something or thinks he has to pay a duty call."

"Grandfather! That's not true," said Kiran, as she pulled up a woven wicker stool and sat down. "Everyone loves you. You know they do."

"Nobody wants a useless old man around, Kiran," said Grandfather with a sad smile. "But let's forget about me and talk about you. Why is my little yellow balloon about to burst?"

"Grandfather, my clothes aren't yellow, they're orange," said Kiran. "I'm going to wear my pink ones tomorrow when we walk to Nurpur to church. I'll take these orange ones along to wear when I help in the work on the new church. We're going to stay at Mama's cousin's for Sunday, Monday, Tuesday, and Wednesday. Baby is going to have his first Easter and Old Grandmother will take him in Neighbor's bullock cart and he'll have donkey beads to play with on the way. Won't it be fun to be at Nurpur for four days?"

"Kiran, Kiran, don't let all the air out of my little

56

balloon at once. Nurpur, bullock carts, donkey beads, and work on the church! First I want to hear about your going to Nurpur," said Grandfather.

"First I want to tell you about the donkey beads. May I?" asked Kiran.

"Go ahead before you explode," said Grandfather.

Kiran told Grandfather the story of Young Uncle's giving her the money, of how the beads were lost, and how they were found again on the horns of the buffalo. Grandfather laughed and laughed when Kiran made a face and lifted her head just like the buffalo's head coming out of the water.

"Now may I hear about your staying at Nurpur?" asked Grandfather.

"Yes, Grandfather, of course," said Kiran. And she told him of the young students, boys and girls, who would be coming out from the city to help at Nurpur during their vacation from high school.

"Girls coming, too?" asked Grandfather, amazed. "What is the world coming to? When I was young, women stayed inside their inner courtyards and never even saw the street in front of their own homes. Well, well, times certainly have changed. And what can these city girls do to help a village church? They'll just laugh at a place like Nurpur."

"Laugh at Nurpur! Why should they? Nurpur is a wonderful place. Don't you think so, Grandfather?" asked Kiran.

"Nurpur is a nice little village, Kiran, but it has not always been as it is today," said Grandfather. "I remember when it was not called Nurpur, 'The Village of Light,' but Giddar Pindi, 'Home of Jackals.' Kiran, did you know that I was the first Christian in all this part of the country?"

Kiran thought about it for a moment. Then she asked, "What was it like before you were a Christian, Grandfather?"

Grandfather thought a moment. Then he lifted his elbows and put his hands in his lap with his finger tips together. This was the way Grandfather always sat when he was telling a story.

"Here in Sherpur, when I was a boy, there were many Muslims and a few Hindus," Grandfather began. "As you know, our family was a Brahmin family, the highest caste group of Hindus. Today, the laws of India will not allow one group of people to be higher than another. This is a good thing, and some day all of this looking down on one caste and looking up to another caste will pass from our country. But in my day, all Brahmins were considered to be very high and holy.

58

"My father and mother were very religious people," Grandfather went on. "My father was a priest in the small Hindu temple by the mango grove. I was an only son, beloved by my parents. Since I was an only son, it was expected that I would be priest in that temple when my father died."

Kiran had passed the Hindu temple often. It was covered with strange carvings that frightened her a little. To think of her own grandfather going to that temple as a little boy!

"Each day I went there and laid my flowers and my offerings upon the altar. But I was not happy," said Grandfather. "You see, my father and my mother had taught me to look for what is true, but I could not find anything that seemed to me to be true and right."

"So what did you do?" asked Kiran.

"I decided to leave home and search for truth in the holy places of India," Grandfather replied. "I traveled high up into the snow-covered mountains, where the cold, bitter winds sweep down from the passes. I knelt beside holy rivers. I visited beautiful temples and saw beautiful tombs. I studied each religion, but I did not find what I was looking for. At last I returned to Sherpur. I was sick at heart, and I thought God had failed me.

"Not many days after my return, I heard that a man, an Indian from far-off Bengal, was preaching on the streets of Nurpur—Giddar Pindi, it was called then. I went at once to hear him. He told of a God who loves everyone, and of his son, Jesus. He read from a book he called the Bible. The first words I heard him speak were Jesus' words from the eleventh chapter of Matthew."

Grandfather picked up his Bible, put on his glasses, and read, "Come to me, all who labor and are heavy-laden, and I will give you rest . . . for I am gentle and lowly in heart, and you will find rest for your souls."

"When I heard those words," said Grandfather, "when I thought of God as gentle and lowly, coming down to seek man, I knew that I had found one who could show me the way to truth. Not long after that I accepted Christ as my Lord and I asked to be baptized."

Grandfather closed his Bible, took off his glasses, and laid them on the window ledge. He was so quiet that Kiran thought he had finished his story. Then he said, "Kiran, the people of this village were so angry that they tried to kill me. They threw sharp stones at me because I had turned my back on the religion of my fathers. I escaped from the village and went far away to a Christian seminary. There I studied to become a pastor.

"In the meantime, the man from Bengal went on preaching in Nurpur. Other people became Christians and when the time came to call a pastor, they decided to call your grandfather. And now we are finishing the new church—a church with a bell to call all people to God. I hope I will hear the bell when it rings. I remember the bells on the church at the seminary."

This time Grandfather had finished his story. Kiran sat very still, thinking about what he had said.

Finally Grandfather patted her head and said, "Run along, little one, the air is all out of my yellow—my orange balloon. Tell your aunt that I am ready now for my tea."

6

THE ACCIDENT

It was the most wonderful Easter Kiran had ever had. Before anyone else was awake, Kiran took the beads from their hiding place in the corner of her bed and quietly laid them on the pillow between Mama and Baby. She wanted Baby to see them as soon as he woke up.

When Baby saw those bright-colored beads, he was so surprised that he just looked at them and blinked. Then he reached over, picked up the beads, and tried to put the red one into his mouth.

But that was only one of the surprises that Easter morning. After breakfast Papa went out and when he came back he had something in his hand.

"I think we'll take Old Buffalo to Nurpur with us," he said. "Kiran can take care of her and see that she doesn't wander off the road."

Kiran's mouth flew open in amazement. "Old Buffalo to Nurpur! Oh, no, that will spoil the whole day," she thought.

But Papa had burst out laughing. "I don't think you'll have any trouble with her," he said. "Here, take her." And he gave Kiran a small piece of wood.

Kiran took the piece of wood over to the light of the fire so that she could see it more clearly. It was a buffalo, but one carved of wood and so small that it just fitted in her hand. Small as it was, it looked exactly like Old Buffalo—the same crooked horn, the same squinty eyes, the same ugly snout. And there, draped over one eye, were the beginnings of the tiniest of carved donkey beads.

"Oh, Papa, you're wonderful!" said Kiran, as she threw her arms around his neck.

"I have more carving to do on the beads and the whole thing needs polishing and smoothing, but I didn't have time to do a finished job. I've started one for Baby, too, because I knew you'd be unhappy if I didn't. Here, Baby, and don't eat the whole buffalo at one sitting."

"I'm going to run over and show mine to Grandfather," said Kiran.

Grandfather was out in the courtyard, looking up at the sky to see what kind of day it was going to be.

"Yes, Kiran, I know all about your surprise," he said. "Your father worked late last night. I don't see how he makes those pieces of wood look so real."

Neighbor came early to pick up Old Grandmother and Baby and Grandfather, who were going to Nurpur in his bullock cart. Then, very soon, singing could be heard in the distance. It got louder and louder as the procession drew near. Kiran and the rest of her family joined the other villagers as they all walked along, singing to the lilt of the drums.

Everything about the trip to Nurpur was perfect. It was cool in the early morning, and they reached the stretch of road shaded by large trees before the heat of the day. They didn't see the elephant this time, but that was not surprising. Papa hadn't ever seen an elephant on the road except that once when the *sadhu* was riding it. But there were lots of elephants in South India, he told Kiran.

Once during their trip, they all sang the hymn Mama had taught her. "He is risen! Christ is risen! Sing, ye happy people, sing!"

As they walked along, Kiran thought, "Now I have Papa and Mama alone, just we three walking together. But I miss Baby. It will be lots of fun when Baby is big enough to walk to Nurpur with us."

Everything about the church service at Nurpur was perfect, too. Mama and Baby and Aunty, Old Grandmother and the cousins sat on one side of the church with the women, and Papa sat with Grandfather on the men's side. Only the front half of the church was finished, and it was crowded with the many people who had come to the Easter service.

But Kiran sat where she could see everything. She sat on the floor right under the pulpit, where large rugs had been spread for all the children. Her family were in the front row just behind her. Part of the time she held Baby or let him crawl on the rug. The other children let him climb over their legs. He played with his beads, too, and was very happy on his first Easter in church.

The choir from the mission school in Nurpur sang a hymn in English, which Kiran couldn't understand, and then they sang one in their own Indian language. Kiran decided she would ask Mama to teach it to her when they got back to Sherpur.

When the pastor got up to give the children's sermon, he walked down from the pulpit and stood near Kiran.

"Sometimes people are cross and mean to you," he began.

"Aunty is cross and Ganga Ram is mean to me," thought Kiran, as she listened closely to every word he said.

"How can you children make such people stop being cross and mean? How can you get them to love you?" the pastor went on. "There are two things you can do: the first is to pray for these people, and the second is quietly to love them. Yes, children, you may not even have to say a word. All you will have to do is to look at them and love them. It won't be easy, because you must really love, and it won't be done in a moment. It may take a long, long time. Try it some time. You will see an Easter miracle. You will see the stone rolled away from people's hearts."

"Maybe I will try it," thought Kiran. "I'll try it with cross Aunty, but I won't try it with Ganga Ram. Love him? Ugh!"

After church, they all went back to Cousin's house. Cousin was a happy old lady who had a hard time getting around because she was so fat. Two of her young nieces were living with her at the time, because they were attending the mission school at Nurpur. Kiran had seen them singing in the choir.

"Come in, come in," said Cousin as the family got to the door. "It certainly is good to have you here."

66

Soon the grownups were busily talking. Kiran went out to the courtyard to find the two nieces. They were showing each other the new bangle bracelets Cousin had bought for them, but they were shy with Kiran and stopped talking when she came near.

Mama entered the courtyard with Baby. "Here, take him a while, Kiran," said Mama. "I want to help Cousin with the dinner."

"Oh, what beautiful beads he has!" said one of the nieces. Soon they were playing with Baby and talking with Kiran, and in no time at all, dinner was ready. It was a delicious meal of hot meat curry, peas with little squares of fried milk curds, and rice made golden with saffron powder.

Yes, Easter was a perfect day.

"Two happy days, one right after another," thought Kiran when she woke up next morning. For this was the first day of the work camp. After a breakfast of corn cakes left over from the night before, they all walked over to the church. There they met Father and Grandfather.

Suddenly they heard a terrible snorting and grinding and hurried out to the road to see what was making the frightful noise. The dust was flying as high as the trees as two jeeps came into sight. The first one was the city pastor's jeep. It was filled with very pretty girls wearing colorful saris. They called out a greeting as they drove into the church yard.

"Oh, wouldn't it be fun to wear a sari and ride in a jeep!" said Kiran.

"Umph!" grumbled Grandfather. "Well, I never in my life expected to see young women riding around on a motor and then going to work with men on a Christian church. What is the world coming to? These young women should be home behind walls, where they belong."

"Mama isn't home behind a wall, Grandfather," said Kiran.

"Your mother is different," said Grandfather.

Now the second jeep was driving into the yard. Schoolmaster was at the wheel. The jeep was so full of boys that they were hanging onto the sides of it and clinging to the top.

Soon everyone was at work. A huge iron pot filled with water for tea had already been set up on stones and a fire lit under it. Fathers were carrying lumber or hammering boards together to make more benches. The young men were everywhere—carrying heavy beams to support the roof, sawing, pounding, climbing up on rafters. The children were picking up broken bits of dried brick and sweeping and cleaning the yard.

The girls from the city were busy helping the village women plaster the floor of the finished part of the church. They were mixing paints and making beautiful designs on the walls. One of them was adding fuel cakes to the fire to keep the tea boiling; and another, who wore a red sari, was just bringing a tumbler of tea to Grandfather as Kiran ran up to ask him to hold her wooden buffalo so she could work better. Grandfather was sitting in a chair in the center of all the activity. He was turning his head this way and that, watching everything that was going on.

"Grandfather, sir," said the girl in the beautiful red sari—she spoke very politely—"may I give you a tumbler of tea?"

"Thank you," said Grandfather. "It is very kind of you. I've been watching you girls from the city. You certainly know how to work."

"We are doing this for God, sir, and it is happy work," the girl replied. And she went back to her tea-making.

"Mama is over by the plastering," said Kiran, "but I can't find Papa."

"He has just left for the blacksmith shop to get some of the tools fixed," said Grandfather.

The pastor was planting a hedge at one side of the church yard. When Kiran got tired of picking up broken bricks, she went over to watch him.

"Good morning, Kiran," said the pastor. "Do you want to help me?"

"Yes, Pastor, sir," Kiran replied. "I'd like to help you."

"Then hand me those little plants, one by one, while I dig the holes to put them in. These little plants have a story, Kiran. Some years ago, we had a terrible flood here in Nurpur. As the waters poured down from the hills, one tiny plant from the garden of some English gentleman was washed into the schoolyard. I found it and planted it, and it turned out to make a very good hedge—thick enough and tough enough to keep out animals. These little plants came from that hedge."

"How did you know that the first plant came from an English Sahib's garden?" asked Kiran.

"Because this is not an Indian plant. It is an English plant," the pastor replied.

The two went on talking and working, and before they knew it, it was time for lunch. Papa was still at the blacksmith shop, but the other workers were all called together, and they sat down under the trees.

The pastor asked God to bless their food and to bless the work of their hands. Then "plates," which were really large green leaves, were filled with hot food and passed around, to the men first.

As they were resting from the heat of the day, the young people from the city took turns telling of their plans for their life work for God. Two of the girls were going to be doctors. Three of the boys wanted to teach, and two were planning to become pastors. One boy was going to learn new ways of farming so that he could help the people of his village, and one was going to a trade school to learn how to take care of jeeps.

"Now it is time for us to hear about the beginnings of this church," said the pastor from the city. "I listened to Grandfather for a long time last night, and what he said was so interesting that I want you to hear it."

Everyone was very quiet listening to Grandfather's story. Kiran was so proud of Grandfather! When he had finished talking, she ran over to the iron kettle to get him another tumbler of tea.

Just as she got to the fire, one of the rocks holding the big pot split in two. The boiling tea spilled out over the hot stones. Clouds of steam burned into Kiran's legs and she screamed with fright and pain.

Her long scarf fell into the fire, and in a moment it was one long flame. The girl standing nearest her grabbed a shawl from a bench, wrapped Kiran in it, and threw her to the ground, rolling her over and over to put out the fire.

Kiran heard voices and shouting and she heard Mama crying, but the pain in her legs made it sound far, far away. Soon she was being carried by one of the young men, who was saying, "I'll take her in the jeep to the wayside clinic. The group from the hospital left the city this morning at the same time we did. I know exactly where to find them. It's about ten miles from here."

Mama was wailing, "What shall I do? What shall I do? Papa isn't here. I can't leave Baby. Oh, what shall I do?"

"You look after Grandfather," said a voice that was Aunty's. "I'm going with Kiran."

The next thing Kiran knew they were moving along the road like the wind. Aunty was holding her tightly in her arms. The bumping of the jeep made Kiran's legs hurt more than ever. Would the ride never end? Aunty held Kiran's head against her soft shoulder. Kiran snuggled into her aunt's shoulder and thought confusedly, "Why, she does love me after all. And I

74

didn't do anything to make her love me!" It was a comfort to be in Aunty's arms. If only the pain would stop.

The rest of the afternoon was a blur in Kiran's mind. She knew when the jeep stopped. She saw the strange white face of the missionary doctor as he bent over her. His voice was kind as he said, "She'll have to go into the city to the hospital. These burns mustn't become infected. We'll take her in the mobile clinic bus so she can lie down all the way."

Then Kiran heard the young man say, "I'll hurry back to Nurpur and tell her parents not to worry. She is in good hands."

But the voices were like a dream and the pain was like a nightmare. At last Kiran felt the prick of a needle in her arm and in a few moments the pain had all gone away. Then she fell asleep.

7

KIRAN MEETS LINDA

"Where am I?" asked Kiran the next time she opened her eyes. It was late afternoon. She was lying on a narrow bed in a small white room, and at the same time bumping through space at a terrible speed. Trees flew by the window so fast that they looked like a ribbon of green silk spread on the sky.

"There, there, don't worry," said Aunty, who was sitting beside the bed. "You are riding in the mobile clinic bus. We are on our way to the city."

"Oh, Aunty, why does it go so fast? The bumping hurts my legs," said Kiran.

"The doctor is hurrying to get you to the hospital, Kiran. There he will fix your legs so they won't hurt any more," said Aunty.

"I'm afraid of the hospital," said Kiran. "What will it be like?"

"Well, it will be a little like the inside of this bus,"

said Aunty. "This bus is really a small hospital. See, here are the cupboards for the medicine, and here are the drawers where the bandages are kept. This funny-looking thing is an X-ray machine. It takes pictures of your insides."

"I don't want any pictures taken of my insides. I want to go home to Mama. Aunty, tell them to turn the bus around and take me back to Mama," said Kiran, and she began to cry.

"Kiran, don't cry. I have something for you—something I've wanted to give you for a long time." Aunty reached down the front of her tunic and took out two small gold bracelets that were hanging on a long chain around her neck. Kiran had often noticed the chain, but she had never known that there were bangles hanging under Aunty's blouse. Where had the tiny bracelets come from? Had they belonged to Aunty when she was a little girl? Kiran had never heard of anyone wearing her little-girl bracelets around her neck.

They were so small that Aunty had to fold Kiran's hand together so that the bracelets would slide onto her wrist, one by one.

"There," said Aunty. "I've done it at last. I've given you my little girl's bangles."

What little girl? That was a strange thing for Aunty to say! Kiran had no time to wonder any further. The clinic bus had slowed down. The trees outside the window began to look like trees again, and the bus drew up in front of the largest building that Kiran had ever seen. There were windows and windows and windows all over it.

"Oh, Aunty, I'm scared!" whispered Kiran. The back door of the bus opened and the doctor looked in. How white his face and hands were! And what a strange yellow color his hair was! But he was smiling as he took her in his arms and carefully lifted her off the bed.

"There is nothing to be afraid of," he said in her language. "There is not one thing to be afraid of. I have a little girl about your age, and she comes to the hospital every day just because she likes it so much. Shall I bring her in to see you?"

"Y-yes," said Kiran. She wasn't quite sure she wanted to see the doctor's little girl. What she really wanted was for her legs to stop hurting.

The doctor carried her through long halls that were a soft green color. Aunty hurried along behind him, trying to keep up with the doctor's big steps. The doctor spoke to everyone he met. A tall lady wearing a stiff white dress and a stiff white cap on top of her gray hair said, "Doctor, who is this?"

"This is Kiran," said the doctor. "She has come to stay with you for a while. We are on our way up to your ward now. And this is Kiran's aunt. She'll help you look after her."

They all stepped into a very small room. The lady in white pushed a button and the whole room started to go right up toward the sky. Kiran clutched at the doctor's coat with both hands. Didn't any of their rooms stand still the way a room ought to?

"Don't be afraid, Kiran," said the doctor. "This is an elevator. It's a lot better than having to walk up all of those flights of stairs."

Kiran looked at Aunty. She was almost laughing. "It's all right, Kiran," she said.

The room stopped moving. The door was magic. It opened all by itself. The doctor carried Kiran into a large room filled with children—all of them lying in beds. Then everything seemed to happen at once. A girl in blue and white put a glass stick in Kiran's mouth and said, "Under your tongue and shut your lips." Then she held Kiran's wrist for a long time, took the stick out of Kiran's mouth, and wrote something down in a little notebook. A soft-spoken Indian doctor, with a little black mustache, looked carefully at the burns on Kiran's legs while the missionary doctor asked him questions.

As the missionary doctor left, he said to Kiran, "You are going to be all right, Kiran. You are going to walk again. You are a very fortunate little girl. If it hadn't been for the quick thinking of the girl who wrapped you in the shawl, there is no telling what might have happened to you. Dr. Chuttani, here, will take good care of you." He nodded to the Indian doctor, who was now putting over her legs a light wooden frame that looked like half a barrel, so that the bed clothes couldn't touch her burns.

"Dr. Chuttani is a specialist who knows all about people's legs," the doctor went on. "I know best about people's insides. But I'll come to see you. I take care of some of the older people on this floor. And I'll bring my little girl in to see you."

"Yes, do that," said Dr. Chuttani. "Kiran will have lots of fun with Linda."

The lady with the starched white cap on her head gave Kiran a prick in her arm. Aunty said that she was the missionary nurse. The lady was so gentle that Kiran could hardly feel the needle when it went in. The medicine in the shot made Kiran feel drowsy. The room got darker and darker, the pain moved farther and farther away, and soon Kiran was off to sleep again.

When she woke up it was morning, and Aunty was standing beside her bed holding a big bowl of millet gruel and two flat *chapatti* breads. As Aunty dipped the pieces of flat bread into the hot cereal and fed them to Kiran, she talked with the nurse who was bathing the baby in the crib next to Kiran.

"I thought I recognized you," Aunty said to the nurse. "Didn't we start our nurse's training together?"

"Indeed we did. That was years ago, wasn't it?" said the nurse. "You left to get married, didn't you? Is this your little girl?"

"No, this is my niece," said Aunty, with such a sad look on her face that the nurse went on with her work and didn't say any more.

"Has the pain gone, Kiran?" Aunty asked.

"It only hurts when I move," said Kiran. "Aunty, were you once a nurse in this hospital?"

"Yes, Kiran," said Aunty. "Lie still and I will tell you all about it. It's time you heard the story.

"When I was a young girl, my father became very ill. They brought him to this place when it was only a very small hospital. Now it is a big medical college

81

where young men and women learn to be doctors. There were no such doctors in our part of India when my father got sick. That is why we brought him all the way to the big city. My mother had my younger brothers and sisters to care for, so I went with my father to cook for him. He was here for a long time, and I learned to do many things to care for the sick. After he got well and we returned to the village, I talked of nothing but going back to the hospital to become a nurse. My father finally said I could go, though all the village was shocked that he would let his daughter go alone to the big city.

"I had almost finished my nursing course when your grandfather sent word to my father that he wanted to arrange a marriage between me and your uncle. I already knew your mother and father, and I was very happy to be so fortunate as to marry into your family. But I told my father to tell Grandfather that I wanted to finish my training. Grandfather wouldn't agree, and Grandfather had his way, of course.

"We were married after the fall harvest. What a beautiful wedding it was! Two years later our little girl was born. We named her Shanti, which means 'peace.' She was a chubby, happy little girl with tight black curls all over her head. When she was two years old, we decided to visit the city. Grandfather's oldest brother lived here and he had sent word that he wanted to see us. And I wanted to show our little girl to my friends in the hospital."

Aunty waited for a long time. She seemed to find it hard to go on. "We decided to go by train. The train was derailed."

Aunty covered her face with her hands. "It all happened so quickly, Kiran. One moment we were all laughing together and the next moment there was a terrible crash. When I came to, I found myself in this hospital. I wasn't hurt badly, but they told me then that I was all alone in the world. My baby and her father had died in the crash.

"When you were born it was all the harder for me. My heart was bitter when I looked at you, because I didn't have my little girl. Every time you smiled and every time you learned something new, jealousy was like a knife going through me. I wanted my own little girl so much."

Kiran threw her arms around Aunty's neck and said, "Oh, Aunty, I am so sorry! I'll be your little girl, too. I belong to Mama, of course, but I'll be your little girl, too. Thank you a thousand times for giving me Shanti's bracelets."

"Kiran, let go of my neck. You are choking me," said Aunty, in her usual manner. "I'm going to market to buy food for us and to return the millet I borrowed this morning. You behave yourself while I'm gone, do you hear?"

Aunty sounded cross, but Kiran just smiled at her. Kiran knew now how much Aunty loved her. She had given her the bangles that had belonged to her own little girl. Aunty waved to Kiran from the doorway as she went out.

Kiran lay for a long time looking at the pretty bracelets that had belonged to Shanti. Kiran liked that name. Shanti—"peace."

The day passed. There was a lot to see as Kiran lay in her bed. Dr. Chuttani came in with his class of medical students. The girls wore long white coats over their pretty, bright-colored saris. The young men wore white coats over their foreign suits. Kiran tried to cover her face when the boys came around, but it was too much trouble to stay under the sheet, especially when there was so much that she wanted to see. One of the students slipped a piece of hard candy into her hand as he left Kiran's bedside. They went on to the next bed. Kiran couldn't see the other children very well because she couldn't sit up in bed.

Once during the morning, a large, fat, happy woman sat down beside Kiran. She looked a lot like Mama's cousin in Nurpur, and she smoothed her gray hair with the palm of her hand just as Mama's cousin did.

"You are new, aren't you?" she asked Kiran. "Well, I have something for you." She felt around in the string bag she was carrying. "I am the hospital Bible woman," she went on. "I tell all the boys and girls about Jesus. I tell the big people about him, too. Then I sell them Bibles or little Bible booklets if they want them, and they usually do. Perhaps you'd like to look at some pictures."

She made a table of her lap by spreading her knees apart and stretching the green skirt of her sari tight. Then she laid the pictures out, one by one. "Which one do you like best?" she asked.

"Oh, I've seen this one before. It is in the church at Nurpur," said Kiran. "Jesus blessing the children—Mama tells me that story sometimes. It is my very favorite story."

"Very well, you may have this picture then," said the Bible woman. "I'll fasten it to the wall for you, right here where you can see it."

"Thank you. Thank you very much," said Kiran. "I wish Mama could see it."

"Take it home with you when you go," said the Bible woman. "I'll be getting some more. The children in a Sunday school class in North America send them to me so that I can give them to little girls like you. I have to go now, but I'll be back again. Good-by, Kiran." She gathered up her things and went down the ward to another bed.

Aunty came back and fed Kiran the lunch she had prepared on a small charcoal stove out under the trees in the hospital yard. Then Kiran took a long nap. She slept until almost suppertime.

While Aunty was out cooking supper, Dr. Chuttani came in to see his patients. "Has Linda been in to see you yet?" he asked Kiran.

"No, Doctor Chuttani. When do you think she will come?" asked Kiran.

"Here she is, coming in with her father this very minute. 'Speak of a deer, it will always appear,'" said Dr. Chuttani.

"How will I talk with her? I don't understand English," said Kiran.

"You won't have to worry about that," said Dr. Chuttani. "Linda was born in this part of India. She speaks your language as well as you do."

Kiran liked Linda at once. Her yellow curly hair,

white skin, and pink cheeks looked strange to Kiran at first, but Kiran did not feel at all shy with her. The two were just the same age and were soon talking together as if they had always known one another.

"If you could have anything in the world you wanted, what would you choose?" Linda asked Kiran.

Kiran thought for a long time, and then she said, "If I could have anything in the world, I'd choose to have a girl just my age, to be my best friend."

"You have me," said Linda. "I'll be your friend."

"But you don't live in my village," said Kiran.

"We'll have to wish some more," said Linda. "I'll come again tomorrow. Good-night, Kiran."

8

DOCTORS AND WATER BUFFALOES

Kiran had been in the hospital for four long months. Sometimes it was hard for her to remember what home was like. Once she was frightened because, for a moment, she couldn't remember what Papa's face really looked like.

Now that she could sit up in bed, and even get up and walk around a little, she got to know the other children in the ward. Sometimes the nurses would let her hold the babies in her lap while the beds were being made. There was one little boy, four years old, who had been so crippled when he came in that he had to scuffle across the floor, dragging one leg after him. His bed was now strung up with ropes and pulleys and piled with sand bags to keep his leg straight. He had cried at night after Dr. Chuttani had first operated on him, and Kiran had told him stories to make him forget his pain. Now he was as happy as he could be.

And some day he would be able to run and play like other boys.

The little boy's name was Mohan. Seeing him made Kiran think of Ganga Ram, the herd boy. Maybe Ganga Ram's legs hurt sometimes. Maybe he wished he could run and play games like *Kubuddi* with the other boys of the village. Kiran had never thought of this before. Maybe this was why Ganga Ram was so mean to her and to everyone else.

"I wonder if Dr. Chuttani could make Ganga Ram's legs straight again," thought Kiran.

Linda came in to see Kiran often. One day she brought scraps of yarn and taught Kiran how to knit. And another day Aunty brought in some grass from the hospital yard and taught Linda how to weave a basket. The days that Linda came were good days, which galloped by like happy horses. The other days plodded along slowly like old, old water buffaloes.

One afternoon Aunty was sitting beside Kiran's bed knitting a shawl for Grandfather. She had bought the yarn in the bazaar one day when she went out for food. She had also bought Kiran a ball of red yarn and some needles of her own so that she could return the ones Linda had lent her. Kiran was a little tired now, and she lay back against her pillow and watched the shawl grow under Aunty's nimble fingers. She was quiet for a long time.

"What is the matter with you this afternoon?" asked Aunty. "You are quiet for a change. What are you thinking about?"

"I was thinking that if I were at home, it would be time for me to meet Ganga Ram and take Old Buffalo home from the grazing," said Kiran. "Aunty, do you think that Dr. Chuttani could fix Ganga Ram's legs as he did Mohan's?"

"What an idea!" said Aunty. Then it was Aunty's turn to be quiet. She thought for some time, then she said, "I don't know, Kiran. Mohan's legs were not as badly crippled as Ganga Ram's are. I don't think that the doctor could do much for him."

Just then one of the nurses came in with a letter for Aunty.

"Now what on earth can this be?" she asked as she tore open the envelope.

It seemed to Kiran that Aunty read for a long time, and as she read, her face became more and more worried. She gave a long sigh as she reached the end of the letter.

"What is the matter, Aunty?" Kiran asked.

"It's a letter from your mother," Aunty replied. "Old

Buffalo is very sick. Strange, we were just talking about Old Buffalo."

"Oh, Aunty, will she die?" asked Kiran.

"Kiran," said Aunty sternly, "don't even think about such a thing! I don't know what we would do if anything happened to that buffalo. If she couldn't plow, your father couldn't plant enough wheat to sell. Then we wouldn't have any money. And we've all promised money to the church for the new bell, and what our family promises, we always give. Oh, Kiran, let's not even talk about it. It's time for me to cook your supper." She folded her knitting, put it in Kiran's bedside table drawer, and went out.

Kiran lay there all alone, thinking and thinking. Then she asked God to help her parents. Soon Linda and her father came in.

"You look sad tonight, Kiran," said Linda's father. "Is anything the matter?"

Kiran told them all about the letter and then she burst into tears.

"Don't cry, Kiran," said Linda. "Father will go to your village and make your buffalo well, won't you, Father?"

"Linda, I am a busy man," said her father. "I can't leave everything here and go off to take care of a sick buffalo. I don't think I'd know what to do for it any-way."

"Father, please say that you will," pleaded Linda.

Dr. Chuttani came into the ward and Linda's father turned to him, "What do you think of these children?" he asked. "They want me to drop everything and go out to Kiran's village to take care of a sick buffalo!"

"Where is this sick buffalo?" asked Dr. Chuttani.

"At our home, in Sherpur," said Kiran.

"Sherpur. That's the place where we were hoping to start one of our village clinics," said Dr. Chuttani.

"You mean the place where the Hindu village elders don't want us to come?" asked Linda's father. "This might be a good chance to talk with them about it. But, no. I don't believe we can spare the time. We're too busy here."

"Please, Father," begged Linda.

Kiran held her breath, hoping the doctor would not say no again.

"Tomorrow is Saturday and there aren't any classes," said Dr. Chuttani. "Let's both go to Sherpur. I haven't been in a village for a long, long time."

"If you really think I ought to go—" began Linda's father.

"Yes, I do," said Dr. Chuttani.

"Well, that settles it," said the doctor. "We're off to Sherpur in the morning."

"Oh, Doctor, thank you so much!" said Kiran. "Now I know our buffalo will get well."

"I can't work miracles, Kiran, but I'll have a look at the beast anyway," said Linda's father. "Now we must hurry along. I have a lot to do before morning."

"So have I," said Dr. Chuttani.

"Good-night, Kiran," said Linda.

"Oh, thank you, Linda," said Kiran happily.

After they had all gone, Kiran closed her eyes and said, "Thank you especially, God."

When Aunty came in with Kiran's supper, she said, "Kiran, I met Linda's father as he was leaving the hospital. He got off his bicycle and told me he was going to Sherpur in the morning. He asked if I had any messages to send. Kiran, did you ask him to go to see the sick buffalo?"

"Well," said Kiran slowly, "I told Linda about it and she asked him to go."

"Kiran, the doctor is a great man and a very busy man. You children shouldn't have asked him to take the time to go to see a sick animal."

"I'm sorry, Aunty," said Kiran. "I suppose we shouldn't have asked him, but I was so worried."

94

"Well, I must say that I am glad you did," said Aunty. "I wouldn't have dared to ask him."

"Dr. Chuttani is going, too," said Kiran.

"What? The head surgeon in this whole hospital going to Sherpur to see a sick buffalo? What will you do next, Kiran?" asked Aunty.

"I wish Dr. Chuttani could see Ganga Ram," said Kiran. "Aunty, do you think Dr. Chuttani would if we asked him to? And do you think that Elder Bishan Das would let his son go to a Christian hospital? Do Hindus ever let their children go to a Christian hospital?"

"Of course they do," said Aunty. "Mohan is not a Christian. You look around this room and you will see only two or three Christians in this whole big ward. This is a place where many people hear about Jesus for the first time.

"But, Kiran, I told you before that I didn't think Dr. Chuttani could do anything for Ganga Ram," she added. "There is no use getting your hopes up. You'll only be disappointed."

"But you will tell Dr. Chuttani about Ganga Ram, won't you, Aunty?" asked Kiran.

"I don't know," said Aunty. "Maybe I will if I see him."

Aunty did see Dr. Chuttani and she did tell him

about Ganga Ram. When Dr. Chuttani returned from Sherpur, he came to see Kiran.

Dr. Chuttani told Kiran that he and Linda's father had seen Kiran's parents and grandfather and had told them that her leg would soon be well. Then Dr. Chuttani said, "And look, your grandfather sent you this."

And he drew from his pocket the little carved buffalo that Papa had given her on Easter Sunday.

"Your grandfather said he's had it ever since you gave it to him to hold for you that day at Nurpur. He said to tell you that he's been taking good care of her, but she was eating him out of house and home. He

says you can feed her here on Aunty's good cooking. I think your grandfather misses Aunty's cooking."

Kiran laughed to think of Grandfather pretending to feed her wooden buffalo. She was glad to hold it in her hands again. What a pretty buffalo it was—ugly snout and all!

"Linda's father wants me to tell you that he likes Sherpur very much," said Dr. Chuttani. "He says he'd like to live there. Now I have two things to tell you— one of them good and one not so good. Which one do do you want to hear first?"

"The good one," said Kiran.

"Your buffalo is going to get well. The doctor had a hard time trying to figure out how big a dose of medicine to give, but it looks as if he found the right amount. Linda's father and I are now considered great men by the people of Sherpur."

"Oh, I'm so glad!" said Kiran. Then she asked, "What is the not-so-good thing?"

"We've brought Ganga Ram, the herd boy, back with us," said Dr. Chuttani.

"Oh, that is a very good thing," said Kiran.

"It may be and it may not be, Kiran. I'm not at all sure that I can help him. We'll do our best here, but this is a difficult case. I would hate to have him disappointed," said Dr. Chuttani.

"Where is he now?" asked Kiran. The thought of having the herd boy see her in bed almost sent her into a panic.

"He's in the men's ward on the floor below," said Dr. Chuttani. "Here comes your aunt with your supper. Mmmm. It smells good."

"Well, we've brought your young man in," he said to Aunty. "As you guessed, it will be a difficult case."

"Dr. Chuttani, we don't know how to thank you and Linda's father for all you have done for us. I wish we could repay you," said Aunty.

Dr. Chuttani said good night and went on to see his other patients.

Aunty spooned some of the curried potatoes onto Kiran's brass plate from the large pot she had cooked them in.

"I wish I could take some of this food to Ganga Ram, but being a Hindu, he'd never eat food prepared by a Christian, even if he were starving to death," said Aunty.

"But you will go down to see him, won't you, Aunty?" begged Kiran. "Remember how scared I was that first day? And, Aunty, if you see the Bible woman, will you ask her to show Ganga Ram her pictures? Maybe she'll give him one to hang on his wall."

Aunty went off to Ganga Ram's ward. She came back wearing a frown. "That boy was certainly making a fuss," she said. "You should have heard the noise he was making. I gave him a piece of my mind and he settled down."

"He'll get used to the hospital. And maybe he won't be so mean and cross when he can walk again," said Kiran. "Aunty, if Ganga Ram should become a Christian, then he'd be happier, wouldn't he?"

"Knowing Jesus would certainly help Ganga Ram to feel more kindly toward people," said Aunty. "For even if he were never able to walk again, he would be able to face life with courage and know what it means to 'love thy neighbor as thyself.'"

"I'm glad I already know about Jesus. I can try harder to love my neighbor Ganga Ram," thought Kiran as she went off to sleep.

9

HOME AT LAST

The day came at last when Kiran was to go home. She went around the ward and said good-by to each of the children. Mohan cried a little when she told him she was leaving. Aunty thanked each of the nurses and so did Kiran. Then Linda's father came in.

"Well, Kiran, Dr. Chuttani tells me you are going home today. He wanted me to say good-by to you and Aunty because he has to be in the operating room all morning. Kiran, God has been good to you. We were able to get you to the hospital before dirt got into your burns and infected them. I wish we had some better way to help all you folks in the village. You're too far away from us. You need a village clinic in Sherpur."

"Yes, we do," said Aunty. "We never expected that a busy doctor like you would visit our village and we hope you will come again soon. You will be more than welcome to stay in our home."

"Oh, Doctor, do you think you will ever come to Sherpur?" asked Kiran.

"Who knows, Kiran?" Linda's father replied. "If our plans work out, we will. When I do come to Sherpur, I know right where your house is and I'll certainly come to see you. Say hello to your buffalo for me, will you?"

"And if you come, will you bring Linda with you?" asked Kiran.

"Of course," said Linda's father. "And now I want to take you over to our house to see her. We never let her come over to the hospital in the morning because the nurses and doctors are busy with treatments then, and though she said good-by to you last night, she wants to see you one more time before you go. I was called out before breakfast this morning and I'm going back now to have it, so I'll ride you over on the handlebars of my bicycle."

"Please don't let her stay too long," said Aunty. "We have to catch the bus."

"We'll be back before you've finished packing up," said the doctor.

Soon Linda and her mother were showing Kiran their home. Linda's mother had a peaceful, happy face, and her hair looked like spun gold. She also spoke Kiran's language.

102

Kiran slipped off her sandals and walked on the bare cement floor around the edge of the soft, green rug. It was all green like grass and didn't have any designs woven in it.

"Don't be afraid to walk on the rug, Kiran. We all do. See?" said Linda.

"We walk on the rug in Grandfather's house, too, but I have to be careful when my sandals are dirty because my grandmother made our rug. Did your grandmother make this one?" asked Kiran.

"No, we bought it," said Linda.

Everything in Linda's house seemed strange to Kiran. The ceilings were high, and there were glass windows all around the rooms, even the bedrooms. It felt as if you were outdoors. Kiran didn't think she'd like to live in a house with windows—people going by could look in.

"Show Mother and Father your carved buffalo, Kiran," said Linda.

Kiran untied the end of her scarf and passed the wooden buffalo to Linda's mother and father. They looked at it together.

"What beautiful carving!" said Linda's mother.

"Kiran's father made it for her for Easter," said Linda.

"You mean your father carved this buffalo himself?" Linda's father asked.

"Yes, he did," replied Kiran. "He made one for my baby brother, too."

"Kiran, if you ever want to sell this buffalo, I know a lady in North America who would like to have it. She would pay you a lot of money for it. She collects wood carvings from all over the world."

"Oh, I couldn't sell my buffalo," said Kiran. They gave it back to her and she tied it up in her scarf again. Imagine a rich lady in North America wanting her buffalo!

Linda's mother gave them some tea while Linda's father was eating his breakfast. They all drank from cups with handles instead of tall, brass tumblers. They ate cakes that were almost black, with nuts in them. Linda's mother called them "brownies." She gave Kiran some to take home, in a bag that you could see through. Linda's mother put some white cakes in, too. The white ones were for Baby and were called "sugar cookies."

Linda's father looked at his watch. "We must hurry back or your aunt will be worried about catching the bus," he said.

Kiran suddenly felt shy about saying good-by to

104

Linda. Both of them felt sad, too. "Do you think you will be coming to the hospital again, Kiran?" asked Linda.

"Let us hope she won't have to come again," said Linda's mother. "But I know what you mean, dear. Perhaps Kiran will come to see us sometime."

"And could Linda come to Sherpur to see me?" asked Kiran.

"We'll see if we can arrange it," said Linda's father.

When they got back to the hospital, Aunty was waiting at the entrance. She had their belongings tied up in two bundles. She was bargaining with the pedicab driver when Kiran and the doctor came up. The driver was leaning against the bicycle part, and Aunty was putting the bundles on the floor of the carriage part of it.

"You could take us all the way to Sherpur for that amount of money," she was saying. "We only want to go to the bus station."

"That's the usual price," said the pedicab driver.

"The usual price for whom, the President of India?" asked Aunty. "We are just poor village folk. And must I sell my coat to get to the bus station?"

At last they agreed upon a price.

Linda's father lifted Kiran to the seat of the pedicab. Aunty climbed up beside her. They waved good-by as the driver swung his leg over the bicycle, and off they went, the driver shouting and ringing his bell to clear a path through the crowds. He skillfully wove his way around other pedicabs, in and out of the way of people, cars, bicycles, and trucks. He narrowly missed a large cow that was munching greens at a vegetable stand and then drew up before the bus station as if driving a pedicab through heavy traffic were the easiest thing in the world to do.

Aunty paid him his money. He asked for more, and she reminded him, not too gently, that what she had given him was the amount agreed upon. Then she gave him a little more and he went away smiling.

Aunty and Kiran pushed their way through the crowds at the bus station, asking everyone they met which bus would take them nearest to Sherpur. At last they found it, bought their tickets, and climbed on. They were lucky to get seats. Kiran even had a place near the window.

The bus creaked and groaned as the passengers poured into it. The engine coughed and sputtered and then, with a grinding of gears, the bus pulled out of the station and into the busy streets.

Soon they were in the country. Kiran had almost

forgotten how beautiful the world was. The rains had washed everything clean. The sky was a lovely blue with a few puffs of very white clouds sailing across it. Women wearing very full, brilliant-colored skirts and bright blouses were coming along the road carrying shining brass pots on their heads. Their skirts swirled around their ankles as they walked. At a village pool near one bus stop, a washerman and his family were knee-deep in the water, slapping the clothes against a rock. One child was wringing them out and another was spreading them on the grass along the bank.

"Look, Aunty," said Kiran, "the bright-colored cloth drying in the sun looks like the flower beds at the hospital."

"Yes, it does," said Aunty. "But what's that in the road up ahead? We'll never get home."

A bullock cart was lumbering slowly along in front of them. The farmer in the cart had fallen asleep, and it took many honks to awaken him enough to move the bullocks off the road so the bus could get by. Once a herd of water buffaloes completely blocked their path. The driver had to stop until the herd boy could get all the buffaloes down into the ditch.

"I wonder how Ganga Ram is now. I wonder if he has had his operation," thought Kiran.

Seeing the buffaloes in the road made Kiran think of her own carved buffalo. She untied it from the end of her scarf and looked at it. It was really a very precious buffalo. A lady in North America would pay a lot of money for it. "I wonder how much a lot of money is," thought Kiran.

Aunty got up, plowed through the people sitting on the floor, climbed over the large bundles they had piled up beside them, and, with many a lurch, got to the bus driver. She had a long talk with him, shouting to be heard above the noise of the engine. She had a hard time trying to explain where she wanted him to stop. "There, by that bullock cart," she suddenly shouted. The bus screeched to a stop.

Yes, there was Neighbor and his bullock cart. But where was Papa? Oh, there he was, looking in at every window, trying to find Kiran. "Here I am, Papa," called Kiran.

He hurried into the bus, picked her up, carried her out and set her down on the ground.

"Can you really walk?" he asked.

"Yes, Papa, look," said Kiran. And she showed him how she could walk as well as ever.

Oh, it was good to get out of that bus and away from the smell of smoke and gasoline! It was so good to see

Papa again, and so kind of Neighbor to come all the
way to get her! It was good to smell the fields as they
drove along slowly. The countryside began to look
familiar. They passed the fields where Papa usually
worked.

"Look, Papa, the men are waving to you," said
Kiran.

He called out to the men as they went by. The bullock cart went over the little bridge where Kiran had
lost Baby's beads and then turned down the street of
the bazaar. Everything was just as it always had been.

"Oh, there is the blacksmith shop," said Kiran, "and
the cart with the celluloid toys, and the secondhand
shop."

And here was the corner nearest home. When the bullock cart turned this corner, she would see her house.

It was such a glorious home-coming! Everyone was happy that Kiran was well again. Mama had the same sweet mother-smell as ever when Kiran hugged her. Baby looked much bigger and much fatter. Grandfather looked a little older and a little smaller. Old Grandmother was in Sherpur again. Her niece had had a new baby. Old Grandmother brought Kiran a dish of her favorite pudding, made of rice and milk and brown syrup all cooked together for a long time, then covered with a lot of cream.

"I've made your favorite supper," said Mama, "rice and lentils with mint sauce."

Supper tasted so good that Kiran hardly had enough room left for Old Grandmother's delicious pudding. It was wonderful to be home—to be sleeping in her own bed with Mama and Baby near enough so that she could hear them breathing.

Within a few days, Kiran felt as if she had never been away from home at all. Being in the hospital seemed like a dream. Only Linda seemed real. Kiran missed Linda very much. When they were seeing each other almost every day, Kiran would save up things to tell Linda. Now she caught herself saying, "I'll tell this to Linda when she comes," and then she would remember that Linda would not be coming at all.

Because her legs were not yet strong, Kiran could run and play for only a short time, so she spent many hours sitting with Grandfather in his corner of the courtyard. Sometimes Kiran would say to Grandfather, "Let's play hospital." She would sit on the ground and draw out the rooms in the sand with a sharp stick. She would find some dried mud bricks for beds. She would make little dishes and trays of mud and dry them in the sun. Then she would pretend she was one of the medical students, wearing a beautiful sari, or that she was one of the nurses bathing a baby.

Whenever she played hospital, Grandfather would stop his reading and play with her. Sometimes he would pretend that he was a new patient just coming into the hospital. Then he would ask a lot of questions.

One day when the two of them had finished playing, Aunty came into the courtyard. "Have you two been playing hospital again?" she asked. "I declare, Grandfather, you will know as much about that place as we do before you're finished."

"Do you know something?" Grandfather said to

Aunty. "I almost decided not to have you as my son's wife because you were a nurse. I did not think it right for a woman to leave her own courtyard to go out into the world. I wish your life could have been happier, but I am very glad now that we chose you. What would we do without you?"

"What would Kiran have done if all the grandfathers had been like you and no young women had left their courtyards to become nurses?" asked Aunty.

"I know, I know," said Grandfather. "I've been thinking about it as Kiran and I played this afternoon. Kiran, what are going to be when you grow up?"

"I can't decide whether to be a nurse and wear a stiff white dress or to be a doctor and wear a beautiful sari with a white coat over it," said Kiran. "You and Papa will let me, won't you?"

"We'll see when the time comes," was all Grandfather would say.

Soon it was Grandfather's suppertime. His suppertime was different from other people's. He liked to eat simple foods with no seasoning and he liked to eat anytime he pleased. So Aunty and Mama had decided to cook their meals separately instead of all eating together as most families did. Now Kiran hurried across the courtyard to help Mama take care of Baby.

Papa had just come in from the fields that evening when a messenger from the home of Bishan Das, the Chief Elder of the village, came knocking at the gate.

"Bishan Das wants to see you at his house as soon as you have finished your evening meal," he said to Papa.

"I will go at once and eat later," said Papa, and the messenger hurried off at once. Papa noticed that the messenger did not go to the homes of any of the other Christians.

"What can Bishan Das want with you, a Christian?" asked Mama. She looked troubled.

"I don't know. Something about the rents, perhaps. Nothing to worry about, I'm sure," he said to Mama.

Kiran wondered if it could be about Bishan Das' son, Ganga Ram. Had they had word that Ganga Ram was worse?

"Come, Kiran," said Mama when she saw Kiran's face. "Take care of Baby while I finish the *chapatties*. Papa will soon be back and we will know the answer to our questions."

10

KIRAN HELPS

Kiran had not yet gone to bed when Papa returned from seeing Bishan Das. When he came in he had a surprise for Mama and Kiran. The young pastor from the Nurpur church was with him.

"Why, Pastor, what are you doing here in Sherpur?" asked Mama.

"Bishan Das, the elder of your village, sent for me," said the pastor.

"Now, Mama, we are hungry," said Papa. "Everything is all right. We'll tell you all about it after we have eaten."

Mama and Kiran served the supper as quickly as they could. It seemed to them that the two men would never stop eating. Mama and Kiran ate only a few mouthfuls themselves, as they were cleaning up the kitchen.

Papa and the pastor had gone in to see Grandfather

as soon as they finished their meal. Now the whole family gathered in the courtyard near Grandfather's house to hear what Papa and the pastor had to say. Kiran took Baby from Mama and held him in her arms.

"You know how the Hindus of our village never have anything to do with the Christians unless it concerns work to be done," Papa began. "That is why I was worried when Bishan Das sent for me. But what he wanted had nothing to do with the work.

"It seems that the doctors in the hospital sent a letter to Bishan Das asking if they could talk with him and the other elders about starting a clinic here in Sherpur. With Sherpur as a center, the sick could come from miles around. But Bishan Das wrote to the doctors and said it would be no use to talk with them about such a thing. The other Hindu elders would never agree to having a Christian clinic in Sherpur."

The grownups went on talking about how stubborn some of the elders could be. Kiran was thinking about the sick people who would have no doctor to take care of them. She remembered how good the doctors had been to her in the hospital. Then she remembered Ram Singh's wife, when their baby died of the coughing sickness—how she had wailed, "If only there had been a good doctor here, perhaps my baby would not have died."

Grandfather was speaking, "The herb doctor in Old Grandmother's village is a good man, but there are times when nothing he can do seems to help. We need a clinic here badly, but once those elders make up their minds, they'll never change them."

"But they have changed their minds. That is why Bishan Das sent for us," said Papa.

"Well, this is a day of miracles," said Grandfather.

"You see, Bishan Das told them the story of what happened when he was a child," said the pastor. "He saw a Christian doctor operate on a man under a tree by the side of the road. The man, who was very sick, got well. Bishan Das has never forgotten it."

"That explains why he was willing to let the doctors see his son when they came out from the city to take care of our buffalo," said Grandfather.

"By the way, Kiran," said Papa. "Bishan Das is very thankful to you for suggesting it to the doctors."

Bishan Das, the elder, thankful to her, Kiran, a child? This was, indeed, a day of miracles!

The pastor took up the story. "Bishan Das has been very much impressed by the loving care that is being given to his son at the hospital, even though Ganga

Ram is such a difficult child to manage. The boy will be able to stand straight and he will be able to walk, although he will limp badly. Bishan Das told all this to the elders. They listened quietly, and then one of them said, 'And if the doctors come here, we'll have someone to look after our buffaloes when they get sick.' That decided them, and they agreed to let the clinic come to Sherpur."

Kiran thought about what it would mean to have the clinic in Sherpur. Would the doctors come in a jeep? Where would the clinic be? Would some of their Hindu neighbors hear about Jesus from the Bible woman? Would Bishan Das himself become a Christian? Perhaps some day the whole village of Sherpur would be Christian, like Nurpur. And, oh, would Linda come to Sherpur with her father?

Baby wouldn't go to sleep. "Da—da—um, goo," he said as he caught his little fist in Kiran's hair and pulled it, all the time laughing and gurgling as he looked up at her.

"Baby, you're wonderful," said Kiran as she hugged him. To think that she had once taken him out of their home so that she could be alone with Mama and Papa! Why, it wouldn't be any fun at all without Baby.

What was Papa saying? "Bishan Das and two of the

elders went to the city. They talked with the doctors. They found out that in order to have a clinic here, we must have three things. First, some land for the clinic; second, a nurse or health worker; and third, two buildings—one for the clinic and one for the nurse or health worker."

"They cannot spare anyone from the hospital for this work," said the pastor. "The nurses have too much to do now."

Kiran remembered how long the nurses had to work and how very tired they were when they left the ward.

"Bishan Das will give the land and half the money for the buildings," said Papa, "if we Christians will raise the other half of the money and find the nurse."

Mama and Aunty sighed and looked at each other. They knew that all the Christian families in Nurpur and Sherpur and Old Grandmother's village had given every cent they could give toward the bell for the new church. It was very kind of Bishan Das, a Hindu, to give the land and all that money, but the Christians could never, never raise the other half.

"It looks as if we will be a long time getting a clinic in Sherpur," said Grandfather. "Pastor, you'd better stay the night and go on to Nurpur in the morning."

"Thank you. I believe I will," said the pastor.

118

Kiran could not go to sleep that night. She had been so happy thinking about the clinic and Linda's coming to Sherpur. Now she knew that it could not happen—not for a long, long time.

"Maybe not until I have been married and have left this village," thought Kiran, as the tears began to run down her cheeks. "Money, money, money! Oh, why do we always have to think about money?"

She picked up her scarf, which was lying on the foot of the bed, and began to dry her eyes. There, tied in the corner of the scarf, was her precious wooden buffalo. Money! A lady from North America would give a lot of money for this buffalo. Kiran had an idea. Thinking about it, she went to sleep, happy.

But when she woke up the next morning, she looked at her buffalo again and said to herself, "No, I just can't do it."

Baby was awake and calling to her. "Ki—, Ki—," he was saying.

"Why, he is trying to say my name," said Kiran. "Oh, Baby, you're so sweet!" Then she thought of Ram Singh's baby and what the baby's mother had said—"If only there had been a good doctor here, perhaps my baby would not have died."

"Yes, I will do it," said Kiran to herself.

Just then Papa and the pastor came in from where they had been sleeping on the porch. "And how are you this morning, Kiran?" asked the pastor.

"Pastor—" she began. It was hard for her to say what she had to say.

"What is it?" he asked, as he stooped down beside her. This made it easier for her to talk to him. Now she stood looking down into his kind face.

"Pastor, sir, Papa gave me this wooden buffalo for Easter." She showed him the carved wooden buffalo.

"It is beautiful, Kiran," he said to her. Then he turned to Papa. "I didn't know you could do this sort of thing. I've been looking for someone to carve a cross on our new pulpit. Here, Kiran, let me tie this precious buffalo in your scarf for you."

"No, Pastor. I am giving it to you and Papa to take to the missionary doctor," said Kiran. "He knows a lady in North America who will give a lot of money for it. You can use that money to help pay for the clinic."

The pastor was very quiet as he rose to his feet, still holding the buffalo in his hand. "Kiran," he said, laying his other hand upon her head, "God bless you richly for this." And he walked out toward Grandfather's house.

"You've given me an idea, Kiran," said Papa. "Perhaps I could make some more buffaloes and sell them for the clinic."

The next Sunday they all went to church in Nurpur. Kiran had no idea, when the pastor got up to preach, that she was going to be in his sermon. Of course her name was not mentioned and no one knew whom the pastor was talking about, but there was Kiran, right in the middle of the pastor's sermon. That is what he said.

"I had my sermon for today prepared, but something happened this week. I want to share that experience with you."

Then he told the people about the Hindu, Bishan Das, and his generous gift for a clinic at Sherpur that would serve all the people in the villages round about. But the Christians would have to raise the other half of the money and provide a nurse. It was here that Kiran came into the sermon, for the pastor told of her being willing to sell her beloved carved wooden buffalo so that the clinic might be built in Sherpur.

The pastor went on, "When I saw that little girl give up her most precious possession, I wondered what I could give up, what we as a church could sacrifice, that Christ's healing hand might be laid upon our village children."

It gave Kiran a queer feeling to be talked about in front of everyone. She looked around the church, but no one was looking at her, so she felt better.

"When I saw what it cost one little girl, I felt that we as a church should give up the thing we want most, for this good cause," said the pastor. "My people, what are we going to do?" He leaned far over the pulpit and looked down at his congregation.

There was silence for a few minutes. Then an old man in the front of the church slowly rose to his feet and half faced the congregation. "Pastor, the thing we want most for our church, the thing that would be hardest for us to give up, would be our bell. We have prayed for it. We have longed to hear it ringing across our field. We have set aside some money for it. I would like to see our church sacrifice the bell and give the money to build a Christian hospital clinic at Sherpur."

There was a murmur of disapproval, and then some of the men began to argue about it. Some of them thought that the clinic should be at Nurpur. Others said that Nurpur was too small, that the doctors wouldn't set up a clinic in such a small place, that Sherpur was a center for the surrounding villages. Then some said the Nurpur Christians should keep

122

all their money in Nurpur. "Why should we give for something in Sherpur?" asked one.

"What would we have done for a new church if the Sherpur Christians had not helped us in Nurpur?" asked another.

A tall, thin man in the back of the church then spoke. "I was once a Hindu," he said. "This is the first time that Christians and Hindus have worked together for the good of all of us. I know that this could only be the working of the Holy Spirit of God. Here is an opportunity that this church must not miss."

There were a few more objections, but before the service was over, it had been decided that the money for the bell should go to build the clinic at Sherpur.

"Some day we will have strong, sturdy sons and daughters who will buy a bell for this church," said the pastor. "May I tell you how happy I am today to be your pastor? God has led us so far. We have almost enough money to build the clinic."

Then, one by one, the men offered to help build the clinic themselves. One man offered some bricks he had been saving to build a room on his house, another offered wood for the doors, and still another offered tables and chairs.

"Let us now pray that God will guide us to the nurse

or health visitor that the doctors say is necessary," said the pastor. "We need someone with medical training —even a little medical training. And we must pray, too, for money to build a house for this person."

After he pronounced the benediction, the pastor said, "Let us all sing a hymn of praise to God, who has done great things this day." How everyone sang! The church was filled with music.

When Kiran and her family got back to Sherpur, they all ate their Sunday meal together in the courtyard. Everyone was very quiet. It had been a wonderful service, but Kiran was still sad. They would never find a nurse—not for a long, long time. Perhaps Kiran would never see Linda again.

Grandfather was very quiet, too. Then he spoke. "Ever since the pastor told me what my granddaughter did, I've been thinking. I've decided that it is time for me to give up something very precious to me. Aunty, go into the house and get the letter-writing materials. I want you to write a letter to the missionary doctor. Tell him I have found a nurse for his clinic at Sherpur. Tell him I have a place for her to live—right here in this house. There will be no need for another building."

"But who is the nurse to be?" asked Aunty.

"You, my dear," said Grandfather. "I have been selfish because I like the way you take care of me. Now I will send for the wife of my youngest son. Then she will be here when my son comes home from the army, and you will be free to do the work you love. Yes, Aunty, you will be the nurse for the new clinic."

"Oh, Grandfather, thank you!" said Aunty. She quickly knelt down and touched his feet, as people in India do when they are especially thankful. "Don't worry. I will teach Young Uncle's wife just how to take care of you," Aunty added. Then she went into the house for the writing materials.

"And by the way," Grandfather said to Aunty when she returned, "invite the doctor's small daughter to come with her father each time he comes to Sherpur."

"Oh, Grandfather," said Kiran, as she put both her arms around his neck and hugged him, "you are the most wonderful grandfather in the whole world!"

NAMES AND WORDS IN THE STORY

anna	AN-nuh	a unit of money (16 annas to a rupee)
Bengal	ben-GAWL	a region in northeast India
Bishan Das	BI-shahn DAHS	
Brahmin	BRAH-min	the highest caste of Hindus
chapatti	chah-PAH-tee	round, flat bread
Chuttani	chuh-TAHN-ee	
Ganga Ram	GUN-ga RAHM	
ghee	ghee	melted butter fat
Giddar Pindi	GHID-dar PIN-dee	Home of Jackals
Kiran	KEE-run	
Kubuddi	KUH-buh-dee	a game
Mohan	MOH-hun	
monsoon	mahn-SOON	heavy summer rains
Muslim	MOOS-lim	
Nurpur	NOOR-poor	Village of Light
rupee	roo-PEE	a unit of money
sadhu	SAH-doo	a Hindu holy man
sari	SAH-ree	draped dress of an Indian woman
Shanti	SHAHN-tee	
Sherpur	SHARE-poor	Village of Lions

FORMAT NOTES

This book is set in Caledonia 14 point, leaded 4 points.

Manufactured by Sowers Printing Company, Lebanon, Pa.
Paper covers by Affiliated Lithographers, Inc., New York
Text paper, S. D. Warren's Olde Style Wove
Typographic design by Barbara M. Knox